To my Goose and
Grandpa George: For
always loving me.

my goose is unlike any goose in the world.

my goose makes pancakes for breakfast.

CAN YOUR GOOSE DO THAT?

my goose drives me to school.

CAN YOUR GOOSE DO THAT?

MY GOOSE LIKES TO PLAY GAMES WITH ME.

CAN YOUR GOOSE DO THAT?

my goose takes me shopping for new toys.

CAN YOUR GOOSE DO THAT?

my goose serves ice cream for dinner.

CAN YOUR GOOSE DO THAT?

my goose helps me with my homework.

CAN YOUR GOOSE DO THAT?

my Goose Tucks me in at night.

CAN YOUR GOOSE DO THAT?

SHHH.....
I HAVE A SECRET. DO YOU WANT TO HEAR IT?

MY GOOSE ISN'T A GOOSE AT ALL! SHE'S MY GRANNY GOOSE AND SHE'S THE BEST GRANNY I KNOW!

___________________'S

COLORING BOOK

DATE: _________________________

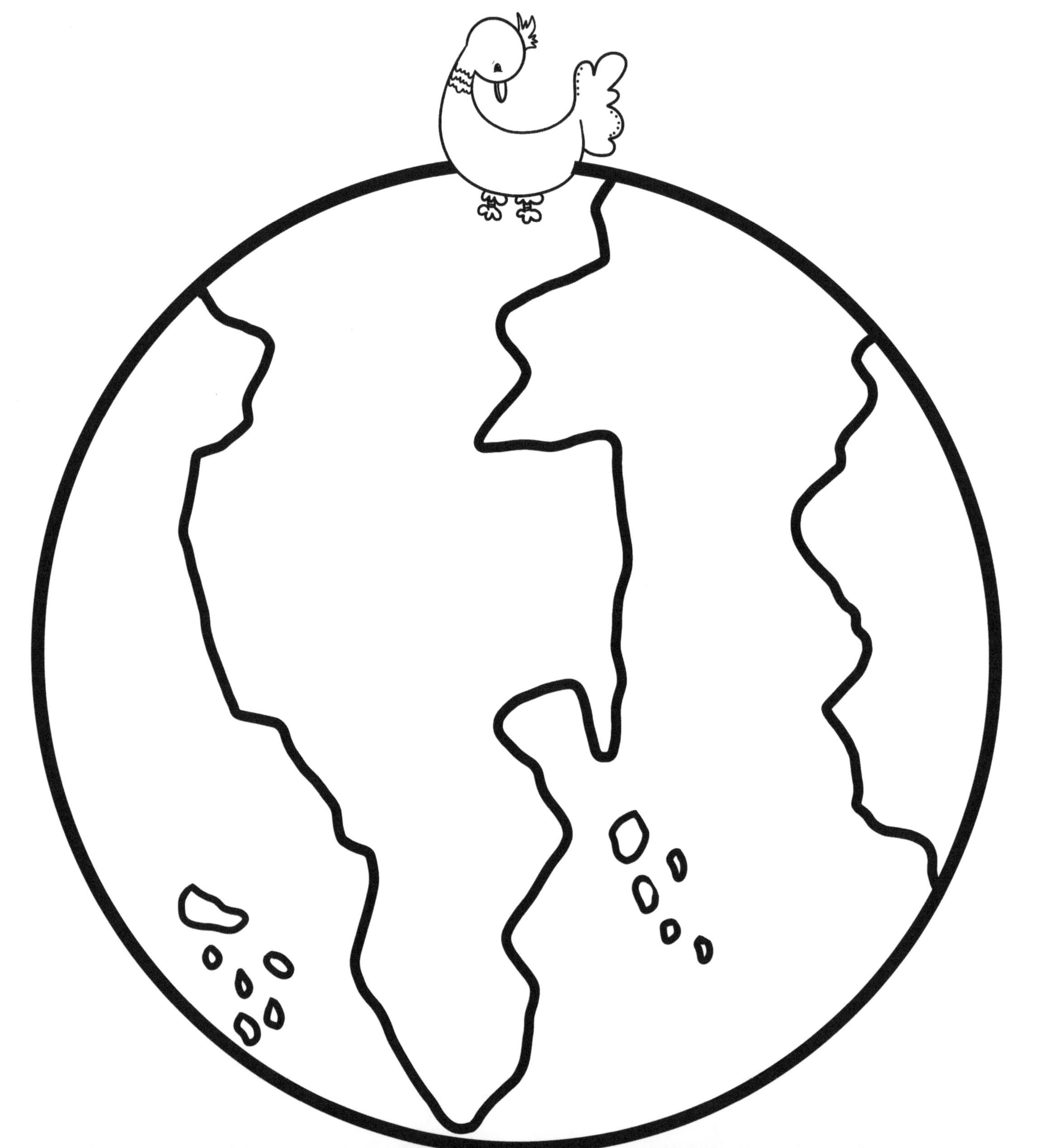

TOY STORE

MATH
1+1=2